Monkey
Mischief

Written by Tori Kosara

Senior Editor Tori Kosara
Proofreader Kayla Dugger
Designers Stefan Georgiou and Thelma-Jane Robb
Jacket Designer Guy Harvey
Pre-production Producer Siu Yin Chan
Producer Lloyd Robertson
Design Manager Guy Harvey
Managing Editor Sarah Harland
Publisher Julie Ferris
Art Director Lisa Lanzarini
Publishing Director Simon Beecroft

Reading Consultant Linda B. Gambrell, Ph.D.

First American Edition, 2019
Published in the United States by DK Publishing
345 Hudson Street, New York, New York 10014

Page design copyright © 2019 Dorling Kindersley Limited
DK, a Division of Penguin Random House LLC
19 20 21 22 23   10 9 8 7 6 5 4 3 2 1
001—314131—Feb/2019

Published in Great Britain by Dorling Kindersley Limited.

A catalog record for this book is available from the Library of Congress.

ISBN (Paperback): 978-1-4654-8438-3
ISBN (Hardcover): 978-1-4654-8439-0

DK books are available at special discounts when purchased in bulk for sales promotions, premiums, fund-raising, or educational use. For details, contact: DK Publishing Special Markets, 345 Hudson Street, New York, New York 10014
SpecialSales@dk.com

Printed and bound in China

www.dk.com
www.fingerlings.com

A WORLD OF IDEAS:
SEE ALL THERE IS TO KNOW

Contents

Melody Village

Welcome to Melody Village. Monkeys, sloths, and unicorns live in this town. It is a great place to live!

Big town

Explore Melody Village.

The Vines
The monkeys live high up in the trees.

Home sweet home
Some animals live in houses like this.

Sparkle Heights
The unicorns live in a
land made of candy.

Clubhouse
This big tree house
is fun to play in.

Monkeys hang out in the Vines. They live in tree houses. They climb up to their homes. They speed down slides to go out. Whee!

Monkeys visit the sloths.
They surf together at Sloth
Beach. It is a nice place.

The unicorns live in Sparkle Heights. Bushes are made of tarts. Trees are made of lollipops. Monkeys like to eat these treats.

Meet the monkeys

The monkeys have a lot of energy. They swing, dance, and bounce. The monkeys can be loud and wild. They all love to have fun.

Bella

Mia

Boris

Finn

Sophie

Zoe

13

Sugar, Rose, Kiki, and Amelia are sisters. They are the Glitter Girls. They have sparkly arms and legs. The Glitter Girls sing together. Their voices are so sweet!

Rose

Sugar

Bella and Boris are sister and brother. They are twins.

Bella is kind. She is a good friend and a good sister.

Boris wants to be a rock star. He is trying to make his dream come true. Sometimes his plans get him into trouble.

Having fun

These are Bella and Boris's favorite things to do.

Bella

1. Bounce
2. Make friends
3. Tumble

Boris

1. Talk
2. Play the drums
3. Be loud

19

Finn is fast! He loves to race.
Finn wins a lot of races.

Zoe swings on branches all day.
She hangs upside down. It is fun!

Mia explores. She wants to learn about everything around her.

Sophie is so sweet! She gives her friends big hugs.

These monkeys like to giggle.
Eddie tells funny jokes. Summer,
Charlie, Sydney, and Candi giggle.
Hee, hee, hee!

Summer

Eddie

Candi

Sydney

Charlie

25

Ava

Emma

Melon

Monkeys are good dancers.
Hop and spin with Emma, Ava,
and Melon. Ava can even dance
upside down.

Busy monkeys

Monkeys are playful. They are always ready for fun. Milly and Willy go up and down on a see-saw.

Milly

Willy

The monkeys and their friends have fun at the Banana Shack. They enjoy banana treats. Candi and Charlie think about what treats to get.

Candi

Charlie

Go bananas!

Try these treats at the
Banana Shack.

Banana cones

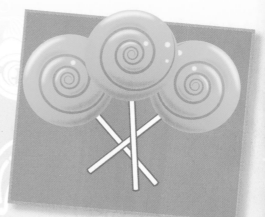

Banana lollipops

Banana slices

Banana milkshakes

BANANA SHACK

The monkeys ride the Daisy-O!
The big wheel goes around and
around. Razz and Quincy will go
for a ride.

Razz

Quincy

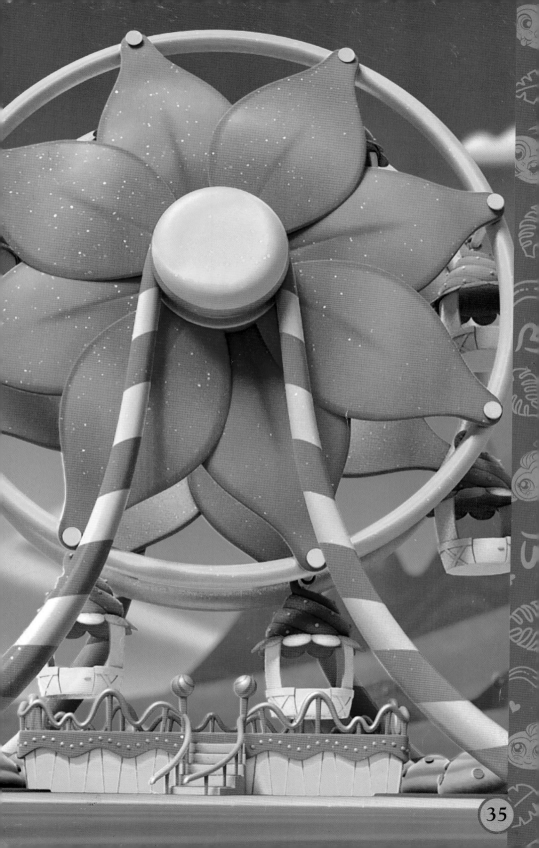

It is fun to go to the playground.
The monkeys can climb high.
Aimee climbs to the top of
the jungle gym.

Look out for the Minis! They are sneaky and fast. The Minis take treats from other monkeys. The Minis like bananas.

The monkeys play pranks on their friends. Simona rides the swing. Liv hides on the ladder. What trick will she play on her friend? Look out, Simona!

The monkeys are tired. It was a busy day. Some monkeys lie down. Others hang upside down. Good night, monkeys! They will make more mischief tomorrow.

Quiz

1. What type of house do monkeys live in?

2. What are the trees in Sparkle Heights made of?

3. Who are the Glitter Girls?

4. Which monkeys are twins?

5. What does Boris want to be?

6. Who is fast?

7. What do Milly and Willy ride?

8. Where can the monkeys enjoy treats?

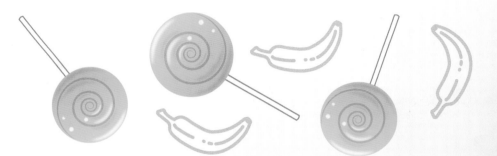

9. What do monkeys play on their friends?

10. Who likes bananas?

Answers on page 47.

Glossary

energy
The power needed to do something, such as move.

explore
To look carefully at something in order to learn more about it.

mischief
Trouble that is not meant to cause harm.

prank
A funny trick that does not hurt anyone.

rock star
A famous performer of rock music.

sneaky
Acting in secret.

tumble
To roll one's body across the ground or through the air.

twins
Two babies who have the same mother and who are born at the same birth.

wild
To have no rules or control.

Index

Answers to the quiz on pages 44–45:
1. Tree house 2. Lollipops 3. Sugar, Rose, Kiki, and Amelia
4. Bella and Boris 5. A rock star 6. Finn 7. A see-saw
8. The Banana Shack 9. Pranks 10. The Minis

A LEVEL FOR EVERY READER

This book is part of an exciting four-level reading series to support children in developing the habit of reading widely for both pleasure and information. Each book is designed to develop a child's reading skills, fluency, grammar awareness, and comprehension in order to build confidence and enjoyment when reading.

Ready for a Level 2 (Beginning to Read) book

A child should:
- Be able to recognize a bank of common words quickly and be able to blend sounds together to make some words.
- Be familiar with using beginner letter sounds and context clues to figure out unfamiliar words.
- Sometimes correct his/her reading if it doesn't look right or make sense.
- Be aware of the need for a slight pause at commas and a longer one at periods.

A valuable and shared reading experience

For many children, reading requires great effort, but adult participation can make reading both fun and easier. Here are a few tips on how to use this book with a young reader:

Check out the contents together:
- Read about the book on the back cover and talk about the contents page to help heighten interest and expectation.
- Discuss new or difficult words.
- Chat about labels, annotations, and pictures.

Support the reader:
- Give the book to the young reader to turn the pages.
- Where necessary, encourage longer words to be broken into syllables, sound out each one, and then flow the syllables together; ask him/her to reread the sentence to check the meaning.
- Encourage the reader to vary her/his voice as she/he reads; demonstrate how to do this if helpful.

Talk at the end of each book, or after every few pages:
- Ask questions about the text and the meaning of the words used—this helps develop comprehension skills.
- Read the quiz at the end of the book and encourage the reader to answer the questions, if necessary, by turning back to the relevant pages to find the answers.

Series consultant, Dr. Linda Gambrell, Distinguished Professor of Education at Clemson University, has served as President of the National Reading Conference, the College Reading Association, and the International Reading Association.

6. Who is fast?

7. What do Milly and Willy ride?

8. Where can the monkeys enjoy treats?

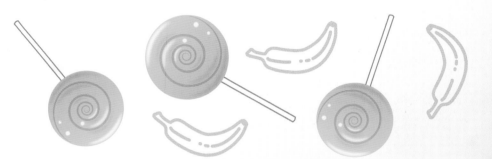

9. What do monkeys play on their friends?

10. Who likes bananas?

Answers on page 47.

Glossary

energy
The power needed to do something, such as move.

explore
To look carefully at something in order to learn more about it.

mischief
Trouble that is not meant to cause harm.

prank
A funny trick that does not hurt anyone.

rock star
A famous performer of rock music.

sneaky
Acting in secret.

tumble
To roll one's body across the ground or through the air.

twins
Two babies who have the same mother and who are born at the same birth.

wild
To have no rules or control.